I0665653

ENTRANCE MUSIC

Stories for Nadira

s{e}an?

Published simultaneously in the United
States and Great Britain in 2018
by Pretend Genius
Copyright © Sean Adrian Brijbasi

ISBN: 978-0-9995277-3-3

other books by Sean Brijbasi

One Note Symphonies
for Emma

Still Life in Motion
*for those who play
Marius and Andréus*

The Unknowed Things
for Julius

The Dictionary of Coincidences, Volume i
for Emma

S{E}AN?
for EM{M}A+

E{M}MA+ the ghost orchids
for Emma

darling two hearts
for E{M}MA+ the ghost orchids

for
Adrian
Andreus
Elijah
Helena
Julius
Marius
Nadira

MATTER

murmur

Contained in this matter and also within the container of this matter is the idea that the first word spoken by me when scientifically I was of conscious mind but practically of none are the arguments or observations set forth below (arguments or observations—they are set forth below).

My mother and father would say to other people that the first word I ever spoke that was not an evocation of the simple coo or a guttural attempt at replication of a random sound heard 'round me was: "murder".

No, it couldn't be. Are you sure? And with absolute certainty my mother (not so much my father) would say absolutely.

Couldn't it be "mudder" or something similar sounding as to be close to "mother", which although unusual for a child's first word, probably wasn't unheard of, and certainly presented better than "murder" to friends and family?

"No, it was *murder.* I was (and still am) a big fan of violent crime and any time I had trouble with any task or my day was going badly I would say to anyone within earshot of me that this or that was "murder". The person who spent the most time within earshot of me was my baby boy. Not that I would murder anyone. Obviously my pronouncements were more nounial than verbial if I can be allowed to speak those words for the first time as if I am also of scientific but not practical consciousness."

However, my father's refined uncertainty (and unrefined certainty, as he revealed to me one night in drunken amusement that he was sure my first word was "murmur"—a word whose (?) beauty he argued had never

2

faded but had perhaps become undervalued by the reading and listening public) led me to believe that my first word might have been another.

At different times in my life I hoped my first word was "Paris" in honor of the rooftops there where one might gaze over mist-covered enclaves and behind their assemblage the soft glow of a sun that looks upon all the world's cities (mostly) alike but stares at this one (sometimes inappropriately). Or perhaps "Lelolah"[1] after the woman whose many friends and lovers killed themselves and who, in the end, killed herself too. Or "pantomime". A word I could never have known and that I have never heard my mother or father say and is ("to be honest") a word rarely found in anyone's lexicon.

---

[1] Dalida

My brother who is seven years older than I am, however, told me that he heard me say "water" the day after I was born. He never told anyone because he thought no one would believe him. But he was absolutely certain ("ain't no doubt") that the day after I was born I held on tightly to his thumb with my *très petit* new-born-baby fingers, looked him straight in his eyes and, without a tremble in my voice, said "water". He thought I was thirsty but wasn't sure if water was something I should be drinking.

So: murder, murmur, or water. One of these is the first word I ever spoke.

this is not the dream i had

The bluebirds arrived and perched on the lemon tree. Sometimes they flew up to the roofs of the houses in the neighborhood which, since I saw them last, had been painted the colors of an eastern thinking.

Sometimes a single bluebird flew to the ground and pulled an insect from between the blades of grass (nestling it in flight to feel the unfamiliar breezes of a new and dangerous world).

A barely remembered dream means that animals (including humans) surround you in ways you don't see. They hunt you from a time when the fur on human skin resembled a patchwork of dread. Animals and their powers to harm re-combined with the human resistance to warm lights (sea lanterns) appear and disappear in the bobbing waves of the sea—

On that summer morning the sun, bright and orange, also arrived—like an orb of fire to destroy a world it learned too late to love. A half-dream of the days of pogrom and the dialogic which, in accordance with the herbs and salts of a riven earth, goes something like this: there are several paradigms to be argued and there are many mutations.

understanding the world

I took my boots off so I wouldn't track snow into the house. I unzipped my jacket and sat down next to the woman who invited me to the club.

"Do you understand the world today?"

The question was asked of everyone in the room. I thought about answering (starting with the words "in my opinion") but stayed quiet because I didn't understand the world and I thought that instead of impressing the woman sitting beside me (which I had done the night before with a long soliloquy about birds over a bowl of reindeer soup and shots of imported vodka) that I would have done the opposite.

My soliloquy about birds might have been enough to withstand the dumbest opinion about understanding the world but I didn't want to chance it because the woman sitting beside me might have reasoned that my impassioned soliloquy about birds from the night before had been roused by the vodka streaming through my blood and not by my blood alone.

"Do you understand the world today?"

It was the first question of a list of questions that if answered incorrectly precluded membership. I didn't care about membership but if the woman sitting beside me wanted to be a member then I wanted to be a member too.

"What about you?"

I thought he was talking to me. I leaned forward and put my hands together between my legs.

"Well", I started.

"Sorry. Not you."

I leaned back. Someone else spoke up. I tried to look as if I was listening carefully but I was thinking about what to say about understanding the world today. I wondered if I said everything I said about birds the night before but replaced the word "birds" with the words "the world" then everyone might think I understood. The woman would know but maybe she didn't remember every word I said and I could change the sentences enough so that she wouldn't recognize that what I was saying was a copy of the night before.

"What do you think?"

"I think the world is in a state of physical and psychological trauma", she said. "If we look at wars as sickness or disease and all of the negativity as illnesses then the world is in need of a surgeon and a psychiatrist."

Everyone nodded or mumbled in agreement. I rubbed her back. While I didn't agree with her I felt that what she said made her attractive to other people (mostly men) in the room.

"And you?"

Everyone looked at me. I cleared my throat. I leaned forward and put my hands together between my legs.

"Well, in my opinion the world in flight are a beautiful reminder of the animal ancestors from which we spawned. When I see the world flying off to gather material for their nest, working tirelessly to finish a home to give birth to their chicks, or gliding effortlessly across the sky I just feel like becoming one of those the world myself and flying hither and thither. Freedom, you know. In my humble, little garden alone I've catalogued forty or fifty the world of all different shapes and colors that come and go during the various seasons. And I know you have to be careful about feeding the world in the summer because they might forget how to find food for themselves but I feed them anyway because I want to see them while I'm drinking tea and relaxing. Maybe I'm being a little selfish about watching the world. But think about it. You can see a greater variety of the world in one tiny area in your backyard or in a city park than you can see of mammals or reptiles in an entire city. You do see a lot of insects but they all look the same to me and I just like the world better."

I leaned back in my chair. The woman patted me on my stomach. Maybe she thought I looked attractive to other people (mostly women) in the room. Someone asked a second question but I didn't hear all of it because I was still thinking about the world.

they only remember the past but we remember everything

I had a memory I wasn't sure about. I only remembered me in the memory. I didn't remember anyone else. I drew the memory on a piece of paper and tried to figure out where the memory took place.

I drew the outline of a lake and colored it in with a mix of browns and blues and greens until I recognized the strange amalgam of hues as a lake (not far from my childhood home) that swirled hither and yonder to the horizon.

I walked along the lake's uncluttered banks between the prickly trees and bushes that otherwise formed its boundaries and remembered it was here that my life and the life of Lelolah[2] Vespertina intersected.

I saw her for the first time as she snapped photographs of an aged wooden dock and the row boat tethered to the slightly leaning dock-post by a length of double braided rope (a row boat in which the memory of an impromptu carnal voyage[3]—consented to by Lelolah—would be invented for friends and foes alike, who might question the memory but who, in the end, couldn't know differently).

She asked me about the prickly trees and I told her that they could only be found in the mountains of Kenya. Children would climb the trees (very carefully) to a reasonable height (to avoid "the vertigo") and watch the fishermen bring their catch up

---

[2] Furiosa
[3] French pronunciation

the trail to trade with the people who lived there.

The fish were indigenous to Peru where I met the king and queen of some royal predicament and who informed me (sadly) that those fish (the fossils of which will provide the blueprint for a far greater and noble breed) were now extinct.

"Sad about the fish", the queen said.

"Gone for good", the king said, picking his teeth with the sharp point of a comb he had just used to comb the Queen's long, straight hair.

street vitamins for baron von yusuf ibn ayyub

The bicycle in the yard is getting wet. I think it's raining but see the kids next door playing with a water hose. The breeze blows misty droplets of water against my kitchen window. It's hot outside but those kids know how to stay cool. They're spraying something down at the bottom of the stairs leading to the basement of the house. Other kids run from across the street. They stop to pick up rocks before hurrying to the back.

{Every person's fleshed out soul sometimes seems beautiful and sometimes seems ugly.}

One night a few months ago I climbed to the top of the tree living between the two houses. I traversed the branches that stretched across both roofs and fell asleep on the roof of the neighbor's house until I was awakened by three crows. The first crow was a southern redbird that strutted in like-time with the rhythms of the Stony Brook Summer Night Palpitations. The second crow squawked (for all to hear) that I was the great-great-great-great grandson of Baron von Yusuf ibn Ayyub (the apprentice tailor of the fall of Rome). The third crow stuck its claws into the back of my neck (resulting in blood filtration) and carried me home. I remembered seeing below me (even in the darkness of that summer night) all the knots and twists of the limbs and leaves of the said living tree.

One of the kids notices me in the window. He points at me and yells out something I can't hear. The other kids stop running and turn to look. I don't move. I wonder if they can really see me from all the way over there.

lelolah (le-lo for short)

I met this woman named Lelolah[4] (Le-lo
for short) who changed my life. I met her in
the cigarette shop down the street from my
apartment. I woke up (late one morning) and
decided I needed to shave because I hadn't
shaved in weeks. I thought just out of sheer
luck that I might find shaving cream at the
cigarette shop. But I didn't. People get lucky
like that all the time and I thought (shoot)
why not me.

"You look like you just woke up", she
said.

She was standing behind me when I
asked the shop owner about the shaving
cream.

"Hm", I mumbled. "I did."

---

[4] Hedda

"Try the convenience store around the block", the shop owner said.

"You shouldn't do that", she said.

"I will", I said.

I turned around to leave but stopped at the door.

"Shouldn't do what?" I asked.

"Need matches?" the shop owner asked her.

"I don't", she said.

She walked past me and I followed her outside.

"What's up Le-lo?" a man who was standing outside the door asked her.

"What's up?" she asked back.

The man lit her cigarette.

"You shouldn't wake up when it's bright outside", she said. "You should inhabit the spaces between night and day and then again between day and night."

"You mean watch the sun rise and the sun set?" I asked.

"No, it doesn't have anything to do with the sun", she said. "I've never seen the sun rise or set and I inhabit all spaces."

No matter how hard I tried to understand I never understood anything. I didn't know if she really said anything that I needed to understand but the way she said it made me think that I had to understand something.

"What time did you wake up?" I asked her.

"Of all the questions", she said.

We walked to the convenience store together even though I had already decided against shaving.

creating in this world is hard enough without the required permissions why make it harder

And then she turned into a robot and I turned into a robot too. She plugged her connector into my neck and we stood on the pier looking out into a moonless night. She pushed me into the water and got pulled in after me because of the connector. In the mirror I see her standing behind me and behind her I see the sun shining brightly on us here in this ceiling-less room. In the front yard my brother and his friends set fire to the wooden micro-plane that crashed into my mother's garden. Japanese children run through the forest of green bamboo—too fast for me to see their faces.

dreams of slam dunking

My friends and I sat underneath the basketball hoop on the playground. We had a bet about who could hit the basketball pole on the other end of the court with a rock while we were sitting down. I picked up the nearest rock and threw it but I missed. We took turns but everybody missed. I walked over to the grass and found another rock. I threw it while I was standing and hit the pole right in the center but my friends said that didn't count because I wasn't sitting down.

I told my friends about a time I saw a girl sitting on a small, broken table in the middle of the playground. She used the table like it was a chair and had to balance the table with her body. I was walking past the playground on my way home and didn't see how long she stayed there. The next day the table was gone and I never saw the girl again. I picked up another rock and sat down.

One of my friends said that maybe she was just visiting and told us that his father told him about an incident that happened in Indonesia where people came down from water floating above an entire neighborhood in one of the big cities there. The people who came down were wearing futuristic scuba diving equipment but when they took their futuristic scuba diving helmets off they were humans and they just vanished into society. He said nobody could see into the water above because it reflected what was below—except you could see right through it to the sun. He threw a rock at the pole but missed.

We asked him what happened to the water. He said his father said that the water floated away after a few people came down. I threw my rock but also missed. We heard a door slam and looked up to see the Math and English teacher coming out of a side door of the school. They waved to us and we waved back. My other friend said that his father had seen the water also and knew one of the people who came down from it.

moving to the universe

In my ships under the sea I have armies that sleep until the times of my signals. [There is a screen in my room behind which a woman changes from one dress into another. I see the silhouettes of her movements and the movements of children playing around her.]

A girl flies a toy airplane back and forth in her hand. The woman leans down and whispers into her ear. I can't hear the words. The girl pushes a chair next to the woman and climbs onto it. The woman turns her back to the chair and the girl pulls the zipper of her black dress up to the top.

The woman kisses the girl on her forehead and lifts her down. She kisses the boy also who has run over to her from the window through which I see the silhouettes of southern redbirds ascending and descending (silhouettes within silhouettes).

I send signals and the armies of an impossible creation and destruction emerge. On the screen in my room I see the silhouettes of outdoor living and indoor living. I see the sofa. I see the lamp table and the lamp. I see the shadow of what I think is light on the wall behind the people who live there. I see the trees outside and someone riding a bicycle. I see the rider's eyes narrowing, his hair painted back by the breeze, his legs pedaling. I see the small of his back as the wind lifts his shirt above his waist. I see the wheels turning and turning.

He dismounts and drops the bicycle to the ground. He hurries into the house without knocking on the door and gives the woman a letter from me in which I write to tell her that I am moving to the universe.

She's reading it now (this beautiful woman). She puts her hand to her mouth and falls to her knees. The girl and boy stop playing and run over to her. They hug her and she hugs them back. In front of me I see the first and second stars of emptiness in the constellation of Equuleus. I see Milfak of Perseus. I see the Pillars of Creation in the Star Queen Nebula.

famous quotes from books by night people

"Even with love in my heart and wisdom in my head, I've been bamboozled by life's diabolical shenanigans."

s{e}an?

"The heart is a tiger province for veins and arteries of other hearts that beat but once per minute. The cannons that fire single warning shots to approaching ships followed above by boobies and below by perch."

s{e}an?

"The lateness of the hour expands and all is being undertaken."

s{e}an?

"Everything I am is all that I have seen."

"The girl fell asleep on the bus. I kicked her foot. She woke up. She looked through the window then picked up her books. The bus stopped. She got off the bus and hurried into Hanami Park. And that was the last time I saw her."

"So this girl falls asleep on the bus and I give her a little kick with my foot on her foot. Just a little tap. She wakes up—still groggy. I could see that. I wasn't sure she knew that it was me who woke her up. She picks up these books on the seat next to her and runs off the bus. And I never seen her again."

the old-house room

In the old-house room—the room decorated to look like our old house—I don't think at all. I sit beside you while you lie on your back between the sofa and the table.

A record plays on the record player. Above us the fan spins. We've set it on slow. It's the same fan we had in our old house and we always set it on slow because a fast-blowing fan isn't as beautiful (no matter how hot it is).

The bookshelves have the same books we had in our old house. I took a picture of them before we moved. The books are placed in the same order in the bookshelves that they were placed in at our old house except for one book which is missing and for which I've left a space between two other books in case we find it one day.

"If I eat a grape leaf from between your breasts it's because I'm dreaming. Sweet bird where have you flown to? Everything you touch and everything you love turns into descriptions of magic."

The rug that you're lying on is the same rug we had in our old house. I've placed the paintings and photographs in the same positions and at the same angles that they were hanging on the walls in our old house. You close your eyes. I watch your face. I hear you inhale and exhale. And the voice from the record player sings: "we don't have to go anywhere at all, we just watch our gardens grow, grapes and strawberries in the summer, potatoes and parsley in the fall".

one of the living

We met outside the music store. He asked me if I collected stamps. I said no. He said he had stamps from Bolivia (Bolivia has two capital cities—La Paz and Sucre) and even Mongolia (the capital city of Mongolia is Ulan Bator). He asked me if I wanted to get a beer. I said yes.

We walked to a bar not far from the music store. In my head I started making up a melody. He looked like he was in a gang so I asked him if he was in a gang. He said sort of not really but that shouldn't scare me. The melody I was making up in my head was difficult to hold onto and it went away.

In the bar we sat at a table. It seemed too crowded for the daytime but he said it was always crowded there. He said he wouldn't normally go into that particular bar because it was in another gang's territory but that nobody would bother him because I was with him and I was carrying a guitar case.

In my head I started thinking up another melody but the music in the bar drowned my melody out. So you are in a gang I said. He said sort of not really. He showed me a big knife he kept holstered under his jacket that he used for protection because a few months ago (at the start of spring) when he was at a nursery buying plants for his garden two people from another gang were also buying plants and they recognized him.

He said he studied botany at Göteborgs Universitet and could have helped them pick out plants for the expected summer heatwave. The nursery felt like neutral territory to him but they dropped whatever plants they were carrying (one of them looked like Red Jupiter's Beard—

Centranthus ruber) and came after him. He had to jump over six fences and run through four rows of Salix caprea (green bushy trees) to get away. Since the nursery incident he thought he'd feel better running away from people if he was carrying a big knife with him.

I asked him if he ever got his plants. He said he did—a week later (later in the growing season though not too late)—but that he had to go to another nursery where the plants weren't as lively and some even more expensive. The melody I thought about when we were walking to the bar came back to me. I thought to myself that I would remember it.

He said he still wanted to go back to the old nursery but hadn't worked up the courage yet. He said that one of the people who attacked him at the nursery was "one of the living" and that he was surprised she took part in the chase. I told him he should have gone back to the nursery with his gang to get the plants he really wanted. He said that only he and his girlfriend were in his gang and that just because he complained about the quality of plants he got from the other nursery didn't mean that they wouldn't grow as beautifully as any other plants.

He said he wasn't complaining about the plants. He was complaining about how the people who worked at the nursery cared for them. He said his girlfriend was "one of the living" too. In my head I tried to repeat the melody that I remembered but it wasn't quite right.

He said she had a tattoo above her panty line (his words)—he pulled his shirt up to show me (right here) near her hip that reads "one of the living". We finished our beers.

He said we should go meet his girlfriend in the park. He said we'd see mostly Pinus silvestris or Picea abies while we were walking but if we took the long way then there was a good chance we'd also see some Populus tremula and Juniper communis that dotted the neighborhood a few blocks away. Well he said and I said let's just take the long way.

panther lily

The address was (even by the greatest descriptive powers of a postman) unremarkable. The postbox possessed more charm in its barely two square feet than any part of the house or yard associated with the address and in my three years of delivering mail to the hidden neighborhood between the town's two broad thoroughfares I had never delivered any mail to the house—not a letter, not a bill, not a newspaper, not an advertisement.

Although there was one time after a few months of post-manning that I put a piece of mail into the house's postbox only to find the next day the flag up on the postbox and the piece of mail inside with a handwritten note on the envelope reading that I had delivered the letter to the wrong address which, in fact, I had done because I had transposed two numbers and got the street name wrong.

I blamed the mistake on my zeal to deliver a piece of mail to the house after having never done so since the start of my budding career as caretaker and deliverer of the people's mail. I thought about my mistake for weeks. At first I thought I had disturbed the person living there—perhaps the small transgression on my part caused unnecessary anxiety or at the very least a harmless disquiet.

I deduced, however, that the person who returned the piece of mail to the postbox had to check the postbox for mail—had to physically leave the house he or she was living in and walk the fifty or sixty steps it took to get to the postbox, open it, and look inside. Maybe checking the postbox was a daily occurrence for the person living there despite the fact that no mail was ever delivered. Or maybe whoever lived there saw that I had put a piece of mail into the postbox and came out after I left.

I decided that I would write a letter (an apology of sorts) to the person who lived there and deliver it myself. After a few days I found my letter in my delivery bundle and placed it as conspicuously as I could into the postbox, pretending to drop other mail onto the ground, opening and closing the postbox, walking partway up to the house as if to deliver a package only to mumble in frustration that the package was addressed to another house in another neighborhood.

The next day the flag was up on the postbox. I saw it from seven or eight houses down the street. My heart pounded in my chest and despite the coolness of the day I perspired. I wondered if within the postbox was a reply to my letter. It made no sense to think that I would look up from my bundle of mail to discover that I had seen wrong but each time I took my eyes off the postbox (to check addresses or sort other mail) I thought I would look up again to see that I had indeed seen wrong and that the flag on the postbox was down and not up.

When I reached the postbox I found my letter inside with the words (I could see them before I could read them) "return to sender" written on the envelope. I stopped thinking about delivering mail to the house. After three years it was as if the house didn't exist. I couldn't tell you what it looked like even though I passed by it five days a week (and sometimes six for the occasional special delivery). And then one day I saw the flag up on the postbox. The flag might have been up for weeks or months or years and I might have only noticed it on that day. When I opened the postbox I found a letter inside addressed to someone in Washington D.C.

[THE LETTER (opened, read, and transcribed here against the law):

Dear blue southern northbird,

yeah it was my birthday but it happens every year so i don't know what the big deal is i got a catdog and suitcase as gifts and inside the suitcase was a plane ticket but i don't know if i'm going on a trip i need to practice my words before i go anywhere i slip up sometimes because a quarter of a century was missing until recently as yesterday they say it must have been painful but i didn't feel anything i pet catdog from the catdog machine my happy family america gave us girls and us boys we named it we carried it we called it pupcat catpup kittypup puppycat dogcat doggykitty kittydoggy catdog so catdog running and jumping fast i can take catdog with me on my trip if i go hiding in my suitcase or grip or bag but i don't know if i'm going anywhere maybe to other maps and famous territories on other sides of the world (?) that have mountains and valleys i can run and jump with catdog if catdog wants to go with me i can ask but meow or bark catdog how do we communicate.]

the boy with the backpack, the girl he saw, the train crash, or did it

I'm reading my philosophy when I see a girl get on the train. She's with her mother and father. They sit further down the train carriage from where I sit. I see her look at me. I think we're the same age or close. Her parents look through a book about The 6 Cities. They're the strangers in this town that I sometimes pretend to be. The girl sits by a window (just like me).

The philosophy says that this moment will happen again and again in the same way forever but I just started reading the philosophy and even though it made sense to me before I saw the girl—to live the exact same life over and over again ad infinitum— it doesn't make sense to me after. What if the train crashes and everybody dies? I wouldn't be the impetus for the crash but I'd have to live a life that climaxes with the consequences of bad machinery or worse some unknown conductor's negligence (to the power of infinity). The philosophy will make sense again (as an abstraction) even though it will be scientifically disproven— over and over again.

[I read philosophy on the train because it better synthesizes with the sound of the train moving and the voices of people and other semi-industrial noises. There are, of course, natural noises from atmospheric dust particles in the earth's multiple carbon layers as they travel closer to the indigenous animal layers.]

The train stops. The girl and I find each other through the bodies that move around the carriage as we depart. Her parents look in their book.   They point in different directions.   The girl trails slightly behind them. I like this family. At the exit at the top of the stairs they go left and I go straight. I can see them while I'm walking to the bus stop (if I don't catch the bus I'll be late for the lecture on Chemical Atrophy of Non-Binding Particles in the Southern Woodlands—the train doesn't go to the university).

After another few steps I'll turn the corner and won't see her again. The world around me is perfect so there's nothing to delay me.   I have nothing to drop—my books are organized to maximize the space in my backpack. I have nothing to come loose—my shoelaces are double-knotted. I have nothing to stumble on—the city sidewalks are smooth. I keep my eyes on her and (as I think that I'll remember this moment forever) she turns around. I see her searching. I don't know if she'll see me because I'm far away now. And then she stops searching and I think that she's found me. For a moment we do nothing and then—at the very last moment of our time together in this world—we wave to each other (a sub-atomic gesture that will be added to the sum total of all human existence).

my best friend is a girl

Ever since I could remember I've looked like someone on TV. No matter how old I was there was always a show with an actress I resembled. When I was a child people mistook me for a child actress who played the best friend of the main character on the TV show "My Best Friend is a Girl".

I didn't understand why people stared at me or pointed at me until summer vacation was over and school started again and other kids teased me about looking like the girl on the TV show. The show was on TV for years but I suppose the child actors in the show grew older and the show stopped. (I read that in real life the boy and girl in the show were eighteen and nineteen years old by the last season and fell in love. Nice.)

I had a few years of relative peace (there were cartoon characters I was mistaken for but not very often) until a show called "The Girls are Alright" became popular. There was an actress on the show named Lelolah[5] (Le-lo for short) who everybody mistook me for. I should have suspected. I had the same feelings (or sensations?) out in public that I had while the "My Best Friend is a Girl" show was running. People stared at me until one day they couldn't stare at me anymore without asking me if I'd ever seen "The Girls are Alright". It was like a dam broke. I'd say no and they'd say I look like someone named Misty on the show.

At first I thought "well this is kind of neat". I didn't understand it when I was a child. People treated me differently when I was older (better). They smiled at me.

---

[5] Emma

Sometimes they talked to me for no reason. I also didn't get the feeling that I was being teased about it like I did when I was younger. I enjoyed the attention during the summer and fall but when winter came and even the simplest errands were complicated by one unwanted greeting after another I realized I had to take action: I grew a beard. People stopped bothering me until spring when another show called "Woman?" started airing on Tuesday nights (it replaced "Girl Music").

I thought about shaving but "The Girls are Alright" was still running (every week at the same time). I kept the beard because "The Girls are Alright" was more popular than "Woman?" and although people stared at me a lot more when I had the beard they didn't talk to me nearly as much. But there seemed to be nothing I could do to minimize or prevent the attention. After a few years of living like a recluse in America I shaved my beard and moved to Sweden where I enjoyed walking about anonymously for several months until a movie called "War Woman" was released and became the surprise sensation of the year (all over the world).

The actress who starred in the movie won awards for her portrayal of a post-apocalyptic war-rig driver who also knew Kung Fu. I saw the movie. She was fantastic and I looked exactly like her. I mentally braced myself for the onslaught of attention I would receive but weeks went by without anyone stopping me in the street and no one stared at me. I wondered if that was because "War Woman" wasn't a TV movie. Cinema movies are bigger than TV movies though (right?) and I should have been stared at more than ever, stopped in convenience stores more than ever, pointed to in public spaces more than ever.

Maybe if "War Woman" was a mini-series on TV instead of a movie? It easily could have been. They packed a lot of action into the movie but didn't get to the cerebral underpinnings that drove the plot. I didn't understand. I resembled the actress in almost every way—eye color, hair color (and style), the flawless shape of the nose, the perfect fullness of the lips, the naturally long eyelashes, the shapely eyebrows, the supernatural cheekbones. Maybe I didn't move like her. I didn't know Kung Fu.

Weeks of confusion went by until one day while I was walking along Engelbrektsgatan near Göteborgs Universitet, a woman stopped me and asked me if I knew the time and then (before I even had a chance to look at the elegant timepiece I was wearing) said I looked like the actress who plays the main character Maria on the TV show "Göteborgs Kvinnor" (The Women of Gothenburg).

stadia 1

Running isn't allowed in the art museum but I saw the painting on the wall by a woman from Ethiopia (I can't remember her name) and I lost track of time. I think I had been running for hours. There were several security guards chasing me but I ran track in high school and was a good long distance runner (I ran the marathon in 3 hours, 14 minutes, and 15 seconds flat when I was fifteen and half years old).

It was as if I was looking at myself running and running at the same time. I saw the guards chasing me from my perspective and from their perspective. From my perspective they looked like they were getting closer to me but from their perspective they fell further behind (slowpokes). I suppose I started in the modern and contemporary section because that's where I saw the painting that inspired my jaunt. It wasn't until I ran through the special exhibitions area that a guard asked me to stop, and when I didn't stop, took chase. I heard him behind me stammering into his radio: "someone, someone is running, running through the museum."

I ran through the 19th and 20th centuries—around the Burghers of Calais, between the Walking Man and the cartoonish monumentals of the Hourloupe cycle where I lost sight of the guards (from my perspective). I spotted them again in the 18th century where I was slowed by the beautiful Madame Le Fèvre de Caumartin whose décolletage I considered to be awkwardly hidden by a common peony and little sprigs of peony stem (oh madame would were a seraph of times anon—or some such statement). I paused for the briefest of moments in the 17th century to take in the Amsterdam Harbor before I raced by a lady and gentleman on horseback (that's how fast I was running) and the curious Saskia van Uylenburgh who looked as if she wanted to follow me into the 16th and 15th centuries.

I intended to run to the 13th century before turning back but I stopped to look at Saint Francis Receiving the Stigmata. I remember thinking to myself "what is this nonsense?" when the guards tackled me from behind.

"What the fuck are you doing?" one of them asked me.

"What are you doing?" I asked back. "I didn't do anything wrong. Get your fucking hands off me."

"Shut the fuck up", he said. "Get up."

"You're lucky I stopped", I said. "You would have never caught me. Slowpokes! Never!"

They took turns telling me that I shouldn't be running through the museum because it's distracting to the other visitors ("you shouldn't be running", "don't run kid, it's not safe—I have kids", "walking is fast enough in a place like this") and that they didn't want me to get into any trouble but that they'd call the police if they saw me there again anytime soon. They walked me to the exit and told me to take off. I heard one of them mumble behind me "fucking idiot" at which point I straightaway said "slowpokes" loud enough for them to hear.

phoenicia

All the girls play double dutch in the yard. I can't see them but I hear the ropes slap the concrete through the opened window. There are dark clouds in the sky and I lament to mother nature to move the clouds to another place in need of water (we don't drink it in the city). The girls should be out of reach of those violent rain drops. I sit down on the arm of the sofa that I helped my father push against the window (he sleeps there at night when it gets too hot). I listen to the ropes slap the concrete and watch the second hand of the clock hanging on the wall. Everyone will be home soon.

the only thing missing is the smoke

The leader of the band played a muted trumpet. The singer stood to the side so everyone could see him play. Through the window behind the drummer I saw the legs of people walking by. I wondered if they heard the music I was hearing. I sipped my drink in the half-darkness of my corner table. The violin music I listened to earlier in the day gave me goose bumps but this wasn't the place for goose bumps. I took a pen from my pocket and wrote down the following words on a napkin: "you can be whoever you want to be".

I wrote them down because I didn't think I would remember them the next day (because of night and closing in). I found the napkin in my pocket a few days later and threw it away.

(The sun was shining on the day I found the napkin. The apartment was filled with the fresh air and breezes of an island milieu.)

A long time ago in elementary school I drew a saxophone in my art class. The art teacher said it didn't look like a saxophone but that it had all the elements of a saxophone (probably in simpler words so I could understand). It was the same day she asked me to spell the word "science" and I spelled it incorrectly. I think now that I shouldn't have been asked to spell in art class but I wasn't thinking then.

{When Nietzsche abandoned his revaluation of all values he wrote his grocery list on it—apples, tooth powder, gum drops.}

I have the planets all around me. I am the festive glow of living and dying material.

I am the embers that smolder in the night as you sleep.

The music was deep in my head. I had become invincible.

i was wrong about her name

Lelolah[6] (Le-lo for short) understood that the celebration of coincidences is a modern phenomenon that exploded onto the cultural scene after being dormant since the introduction of coincidences as a form of entertainment and enlightenment four hundred years ago. Like the coincidence of the man who read that Lelolah was going to kill herself and followed her up the stairs to the top of an office building between 14th and 15th streets northwest.

A coincidence because he had broken into her apartment the night before to thieve from her but instead found a note that sure looked like a suicide note to him—"life is too hard, goodbye forever, fuck you world!". He was overcome by guilt and

---

[6] Carmen

broke down in tears right there in her apartment. Several of his tears fell onto her apartment floor which he rubbed into the wood and which, in his mind, sealed their cosmic connection. After he shed his last tear he put everything back in its place (except for the strange connector device he had purloined—it was the thief in him) and waited outside behind the apartment building beneath her kitchen window.

Lelolah arrived after midnight but he had vowed not to doze off—pinching himself on the most sensitive parts of his body to stay awake. He couldn't see what she was doing in her different rooms but he saw lights going on and off in those different rooms, until finally, darkness. He stayed up all night keeping watch, debating whether he should break into her apartment to save her from herself (or not). But how? It was easy enough to break into the apartment. But saving her? He wasn't sure. He could call the police but that's not what thieves do. Morning came and he moved from the back of the apartment building to the front. After what seemed hours (53 minutes) he was relieved to see Lelolah exit alive.

He followed her. She stopped at a nearby coffee shop, bought a coffee, chatted for a minute or two with a woman who was entering as she was exiting, and walked towards Pennsylvania Avenue along 14th Street. After a few blocks she slipped into an office building and took the twelve flights of stairs to the top.

He reached the top a few minutes after she did and pushed the door slightly ajar to see her and another woman dancing to nothing but the breeze and the distant sounds of traffic below. Maybe they were going to kill themselves together and this was some sort of strange suicide ritual before the end. Sometimes they danced very close to the ledge which made him feel dizzy. And then Lelolah stood on the ledge. He thought it was now or never. He pushed the door open and yelled out ("Alice! No!"). Alice? But she didn't hear him. The other woman didn't hear him either. And he couldn't hear the music.

no one can see the world i live in

Images break apart before I see them whole, fragmenting and travelling along different paths to different places in my body through the small blood vessels of my conjunctiva, before reuniting in my visual cortex. When I first saw Lelolah[7] at the academy she was broken apart into many pieces that each took its own journey through the network of blood-filled canals in my eyes until I recognized her as who she was.

Everything around her came with her and everything behind everything around her came with her and everything behind everything behind everything around her came with her so that all the paths throughout my body could hold no more

[7] Jeanne

traffic until piece by piece all came together again.

The stem from the flower on the table beside her travelled through my shoulder blade. The light brown color of the table itself took a path through my heart. The lace on her shoe travelled along my spine. The kneecap of the girl who descended the stairs behind her wandered along a darker path to swim in the depths of my liver before resurfacing and tracking along my esophagus.

All recombined after only a few moments but I was still behind. Any action moves I took to attack in the world were delayed and any steps I took to retreat left me vulnerable. This was living. More than seeing and more than being but less than living-living.

As for Lelolah—the curve of her neck moved along the uneven parabola of my lungs, her chin navigated the curve of my left elbow and picnicked in the area of my median cubital vein before rejoining the rest of her face, her left shoulder circled my stomach twice, and the tip of her right index finger traversed the distant regions of my left heel before strumming its way along my left side and back up to my brain.

All of Lelolah had reformed except her eyes which had gotten lost somewhere in my body. I asked her if I could see her notes about the lecture on complex memories and amnesia-constructed behavior she attended but she said she didn't take any notes. I asked her if she wanted to go to the Good Times Supper Club and Café to have a drink with me and talk and maybe even dance and she said yes.

demon blood

It happened during the third movement of Beethoven's Ninth Symphony—the *adagio molto e cantabile*. One movement (the 2nd) I was leaning into the old man seated next to me as he tried to tell me something I couldn't hear and the next movement (the 3rd) when I turned to look at him he was as stiff as a board. I nudged him but there was no response. I thought to myself that this is the small world I live in.

I am a small world person, which is not the same as a small town person because small towns are a big part of the world. And not the same as a hidden places in the city or suburb that people find out about later person because hidden places in the city or suburb that people find out about later are also a big part of the world.

A small world as in a world that no one knows about and (I think) no one will ever know about. And even if they did know the knowing not only wouldn't make any difference but couldn't make any difference. A world that evaporates. The old man who died next to me during what was to be the Bozeman's Symphony of Montana's last Beethoven performance of the season was a part of my small world.

The third movement of Beethoven's Ninth Symphony has been often described as the "gentle yearnings of a sunny contentment". But when followed by the intensity of the final movement one realizes that the third movement convinces the listener to lay bare his or her soul—I will take care of it for you the strings whisper— and then during the 4th movement instead of the serenity you were wishing for you are filled with the joy that you needed. At times demonic, at other times merely wicked, but somehow (miraculously) always necessary.

I sat next to the old man during the rest of the 4th movement knowing that the sounds I was hearing no longer penetrated his existence. I didn't say anything to anyone ever about what had happened— even mumbling "pardon me" to him when I brushed his legs as I walked by him and into the aisle after the performance was over but before the applause had died down.

intention tremor 2: faster than rain

I looked through my living room window and saw the lights of the long, black limousine in front of my neighbor's house. My neighbor was sitting in his old chair underneath the cover of his wooden porch. It was raining hard (like soft lead bullets hitting the concrete) but I needed to go to the liquor store as soon as possible. I imagined the bell ringing on the door as I walked in and me shaking off the rain on the hard linoleum as the lady behind the cash register leaned to her right to peek around the well-dressed customer in front of her. I grabbed my coat and hurried outside. I knocked on the driver's side window and took a few steps back so the driver could see that my pants were soaked through—all the way to my skin.

When I was a child I was so fast and quick that I dodged rain drops. There is a legend that one time at a friend's house I plunged head-first into his family's in-ground swimming pool with all my clothes on but my movements were so swift in the water that the water molecules never touched me and after being submerged (for a then neighborhood record of two minutes and some number of seconds) I came out of the pool completely dry. Not a piece of clothes damp. Not a hair wet.

Whenever I visit my grandmother, her friend's granddaughter (Lelolah, Le-lo for short) tells me the story while she and I drink coffee in my grandmother's backyard and I look at her bare, crossed legs sticking out from under her short skirt—the toe-y endpoint of one which always seemed to summon me like an invitation. I didn't know what Lelolah was looking at but my grandmother told me that one time in an unguarded moment over the chain-link fence Lelolah told her that she liked "the cut of my jib" (which sounds funny and which I like) and that I talked like a poet who knew just what to say to "pull on her heart strings" (which I don't like).

"Are you waiting for someone?" I asked the driver.

"No", she said. "I just dropped someone off."

"If you're not doing anything do you think you could give me a quick ride to the liquor store? It's urgent."

She said it just looked like she was doing nothing and probably more so if I saw her as I was walking toward her but that she was actually actively engaged in thinking about something she had done the previous week that if given the opportunity she would have done differently. She said she would have driven off several minutes before had it not been for the rain which somehow kept her thoughts from wandering off like they might have were the sun out to dissipate into the light and join the glow of what surely would have been all the happiness about.

"Can you drive and think at the same time?" I asked her.

She closed the window. I heard the car door locks click. A few seconds later she drove away. I looked at the neighbor who was still sitting in his old chair on his porch and to whom I suddenly felt exposed. He witnessed everything but couldn't know all the details of what was going on (and if he did so fucking what?). I thought that I had already come this far so I stood there and waited for him to look away and when he finally did I took off running as fast as I could. I imagined that when he looked up again it would have seemed to him that I had simply disappeared.

When I returned home I uncorked the wine bottle and set it down between the slow-cooked Cornish hens and steamed vegetables on the table. I thought that even if it looked like I disappeared to the neighbor he would have probably still heard the rain water splashing beneath my feet as I ran down the road. Maybe he even saw me from behind and shook his head.

the animals in my mind and heart

On this evening of music I wish to invite you to the roof of my home upon which I will have laid out all the bedding and accoutrements necessary for a solemn evening-unto-night listening. You may look to the sky and observe the dark flight of birds which accompanies the desire (yours and mine) for something for which no words can offer description.

The darkest flights are born in the sky unlike normal flights which are born on the ground—with the power and acceleration of muscle—before they go on to live above us. Tell me what you need of this music and I will make all that you hear exist in harmony with the world you see. I have no power to do this but I dedicate the sentiment to you and you alone.

Do you remember last summer on the patio during Le-lo's party I told you of the octopus blood in my spine and that sometimes the psychosis of the entire human race collects in the body of a single human being who is torn apart by it all? We played the game of guessing who at the party might be that person but we forgot to include ourselves.   There are animals in my mind and heart. The badger and the crooked little gator (you can see the crooked little gator paws along my blood veins) eat the raw food I imagine for them.

you hate my love captain kirk

I never thought I would write to you about Bruce Lee. I only ever wanted to write about objects and people I considered timeless (hats, balloons, bicycles, kites, etc.). Maybe enough time has passed now since he died. People that we don't know are objects and if they have been gone for a long enough time they can become objects that are timeless.

I didn't know Bruce Lee. I only saw his movies and interviews. I think he practiced all of his life and reached the edge of what it was to be human. I propose to you the hypothesis (that's how I spell it) that humans are unable to create edges. They can only reach them and make other people aware of them and then other people go beyond them to reach other edges and so on and so forth. I think that's Platonic. I suppose that's not a new hypothesis. And in the spirit of Galileo it's probably a theory now too.

People are young for fifteen or sixteen years. I don't know what to call the rest of the time they're alive. In some people, no matter how old they are, when I look at them I can see their faces as they were when they were children. And then there are other people when I look at them I can't see their faces as children at all. This is something that puzzles me and the reason I stare at people for longer than I should. "Puzzles" may not be a strong enough word.

I didn't have to stare at you for a very long time. I shouldn't rate you because you're not an object to me but if I did rate you I would give you a two out of two. I would only give Bruce Lee a one out of two.

I just wanted to say that to you so you would understand how much I like you.

If Bruce Lee had lived longer—for a hundred years—I think I would have been able to see his face as it was when he was a child. But people change. He might have changed and then I would have stared at him for a long time. I'm writing to you about Bruce Lee because I use the ability to see people's faces as they were when they were children for good but I can also use it for evil. Imagine if I was Bruce Lee and I used it for evil.

we shoot at the sun

You ran along the narrow width of the seawall with the torn umbrella in your hand. I watched you from the top of the building as you disappeared underneath. I stood near the edge. I didn't know you were coming for me. I thought it was supposed to be my day.

The rain fell hard on the roof but I heard your footsteps behind the laundry hung out to dry by the people who lived in the rooms below. You came around from behind the wind-blown sheets and shirts. We were cold and wet so we sat close together underneath your umbrella—as close together as two people who didn't know each other could be. We didn't speak.

I only heard the sea and the rain and wondered if that was all you heard too. And then it stopped raining and the sun appeared—at its leisure from behind the clouds—like all the happiness and warmth in the world. And I remembered—for a moment—a sensation that reminded me of love. But it was only for a moment before it turned into something else, something dark. I took the gun from your luxury bag and stood up. I held it in both hands, pointed it at the sun as the clouds drifted away, and pulled the trigger.

i get all the girls

I know the neighbors see the trash across the street. I know they recognize the loose plastic bags and cardboard boxes with the names of various grocery items on them (a.k.a the shit I don't buy).

In the morning I leave my house and go to work. I have to think about dealing with the boredom of being with people but in the back of my mind I can't forget about the trash. I know it's still there (like splotches of fucking house paint on my Matisse).

I sometimes think there are a lot of nice people in the world who I don't like because they do stupid things. For example, I do stupid things (my face conceals this). I make rapid-fire pronouncements accompanied by a series of gestures that leave little time for contemplation. Unable to be, I perform. I contrive a stance and stand like I have a Matisse or like the day of my birth resulted in something more meaningful than the biological detritus of that unexceptional instinct to survive. I barely smile and yet (and yet) I get all the girls.

When I return home I walk across the street and pick up all the trash I see. One of my neighbors comes outside and before he gets into his car he waves to me and says hello. I wave and say hello but think fuck you.

i'm going to kill him anyway

If I see another photograph of a child in the newspaper I will hurt a stranger. The stranger will be someone I've seen before. Someone I've angled up in a way as to know that an aggressive approach will result in maximum chaos and harm—a know-it-all blow-hard with close-together eyelids who looks as blind as he really is.

He'll accept how I've changed him—maybe for the better but more likely for the worse—changed the look on his face and the way that he walks into rooms. I'll hurt him real bad and he'll feel lucky. I've done this before. I know how pliant the human body can be.

But first I'll get to know him. I'll talk about his interests: the currency market, horses, boating. I'll think about his life.

About how he grew up. About how he might have been damaged by someone or something I'll never know about.

We might even laugh together. A genuine guffaw that will make him think that we're friends. He'll tell me about his wife and his kids and he'll seem different from how I think about him. I'll have doubts. Maybe (I'll think out loud as I pace my small but pricey flat) I'll just hurt him—change the look on his face and the way he walks into rooms. It's possible that if we lived in a different time and place that he and I might have become friends.

Maybe I'll wake up on one of those days that (for reasons I don't understand) all the goodness and beauty of the world offers itself up to me, as if to convince me to go on for another day, another week, another month—a day of redemption. And he might be a part of that day but I'm going to kill him anyway.

exit music for rarely occurring events

I'm arguing with someone about which of two wrong answers is more wrong. Both answers have the same question and both answers, according to a "new theoretical framework that explains the risk of rare events", are incorrect. Wrong is the word I like to use but incorrect is another word that conveys a similar meaning in the right (or correct) context. Right is the word I like to use. Answer one is simple: junkies stick needles in their arms even when children play nearby. Answer two is complex: prostitutes pull their recently washed leggings up to their thighs (I see them washing and drying their clothes at the coin laundry near the cigarette shop).

All of this occurs (or will occur?) in front of the primary school where, along with book learning, the children play games on the surrounding concrete. Concrete is an adult substance whereas grass is for children. The softness of the grass is gentle on the children's knees and elbows. "Unbruised" you say but concrete delivers lasting memories of the times little juniors of both genders fell and scraped themselves here (you point to your elbow) and there (pointing again to your knee) but who happily played out their last few minutes of recess (the seriousness of a child at play, etc. etc.), unaware of the blood and DNA they left behind for the rain and wind to carry to places they have never been (and might never see) to mix with the blood and DNA of other people and animals of a darker frontier (and whose blood and DNA have been carried to them).

There is a frontier out there that has soft grass I argue, where hills seem made for children to roll down unharmed by concrete, and the glow of the sun from behind those hills mask their adorable little faces with the shine of life. I think I've won because she's getting angry. But she waves me off and says that I'm drunk again and that I should just fuck off if I don't have any money.

sad life happy

Apparently she killed herself in the room upstairs while we were downstairs complaining about the salmon in the buffet line. I heard they found her in the bathtub naked, wrists slit. I guess she bled out. She was a beautiful woman. Don't know why she did it. Didn't really know her that well.

I remember something that happened to me a long time ago. I never told you because I'd completely forgotten about it until now. I mean completely. Hearing about what happened upstairs just shocked the memory onto the surface from deep in my brain. Like when lightning strikes a lake and all the dead fish float to the top (I know that doesn't happen in "real life").

The only thing is that this fish—this memory—wasn't as dead as I thought it was but I had forgotten it so much that when I remembered it I had to make sure it was really one of my memories and not something someone else told me or something that I read in a book. But it was mine.

I was young, driving to the record store because—I don't know—probably something about a new band or a new album I read about in a magazine. I saw this woman hitchhiking and for whatever reason—I haven't done it since and you'll understand why after I tell you—I stopped the car.

She opened the door and sat in the passenger seat without saying a word. I didn't even have a chance to roll down the window. I barely asked her where she wanted to go—like I drew my words in the air with a piece of broken crayon instead of speaking them. She didn't want to go far. It would have taken her five minutes to walk but I didn't understand distance when I was young (as if I understand it any better now).

I drove her to her destination and stopped the car. She gathered her little bag of stuff up in her lap, opened the door, and sat there looking at her hands. I was about to say something to her about my friends waiting for me but before I did she got out of the car and said "don't grow up bitter". She pushed the door shut. Don't grow up bitter. That was it. And I said "okay". I couldn't think of anything else to say. She wouldn't have heard me anyway. But I remember now that she was a beautiful woman too.

I drove to the record store. When I got there I walked around to the other side of the car and opened and closed the passenger door to make sure it was completely shut. I went inside and started (like I always did) from Z and worked my way backwards.